THIS BOOK BELONGS TO

For Arthur and Matilda. Thanks for letting me tell your story. — SS

For Zoe. — ST

THE CAT FROM MUZZLE

A high-country cat's incredible walk home

Written by
Sally Sutton

Illustrated by
Scott Tulloch

Dwayne is tough. His claws are sharp.
His paws are made to roam.
A rumble-tumble tabby cat
who always comes back home.

He loves the Muzzle's bleating sheep,
the snowy, blowy breeze,
the gentle cows, the cluck-cluck chooks,
the buzzing mountain bees.

On moving day, they left the farm.
They took a tiny plane.
But guess who didn't want to go?
The Muzzle cat, big Dwayne.

Oh, how he howled, high in the sky,

MIAOW,
MIAOW,
MIAOW!

Kaikoura's not where I belong.
I WANT TO GO HOME NOW!

Dwayne's new house was big and bright, but did he like it? **NO!**

He swished his twitchy tomcat tail.
So long! I've gotta go!

He walked

and walked

and walked

and walked,

until his paws were sore.

He walked
for hours.

He walked
for days,

and then he walked some more.

His tummy rumble-grumble-growled.

He needed food, and fast.

A BIRD?

A RAT?

A friendly hunter shared his fire.
"Hey puss, come live with me!"
No thanks, the tabby seemed to say.
There's somewhere I must be . . .

I miss the Muzzle's bleating sheep,
the snowy, blowy breeze,
the gentle cows, the cluck-cluck chooks,
the buzzing mountain bees.

He climbed so high, he reached the snow.
Oh, how he shook and shivered!

His teeth clap-clapped.
His poor ears froze.
His wiry whiskers quivered.

But on he walked, and on, and on,
right down the mountainside.

OH NO! Watch out! A savage pig!
Quick, run! Scat, cat! GO HIDE!

One day, he reached the riverbank.
He stood there, at a loss.

The mighty Clarence rushed and roared . . .
But how to get across?

"Hey puss! Jump on!" a rafter called.
"We'll travel far and wide!"
The tabby seemed to shake his head:
Just to the other side.

I miss the Muzzle's bleating sheep,
the snowy, blowy breeze,
the gentle cows, the cluck-cluck chooks,
the buzzing mountain bees.

How tired he felt! But look — what luck!
A strong and friendly horse!

"Where shall I take
you, kitty cat?"

I'm going home, of course.

Dwayne jumped off as darkness fell.
Night never seemed to end.

He walked and walked till morning light,
and then he turned a bend . . .

AT LAST!

The Muzzle's bleating sheep!
The snowy, blowy breeze!
The gentle cows, the cluck-cluck chooks!
The buzzing mountain bees!

Dwayne is tough. His claws are sharp.
His paws are made to roam.
A rumble-tumble tabby cat . . .

Who **ALWAYS** comes
back home.

DWAYNE

is a real cat who made an epic, five-week journey from Kaikoura all the way back to his home on the remote Muzzle Station in Southern Marlborough. We can only imagine what he did and who he met — but we know he must have gone over the Seaward Kaikoura Range, where the lowest saddle is 1300 metres, as well as crossing the Clarence River. Was it worth it? You bet!

HOME, SWEET HOME!

PUFFIN

UK | USA | Canada | Ireland | Australia
India | New Zealand | South Africa | China

Puffin is an imprint of the Penguin Random House group of companies, whose addresses can be found at global.penguinrandomhouse.com.

 Penguin Random House New Zealand

First published by
Penguin Random House New Zealand, 2019

10 9 8 7 6 5 4 3 2 1

Text © Sally Sutton, 2019
Illustrations © Scott Tulloch, 2019

Our thanks to the Redferns, the Nimmos and Dwayne.

Design by Rachel Clark © Penguin Random House New Zealand
Photo of Dwayne © Derek Morrison
Prepress by Image Centre Group
Printed and bound in China by RR Donnelley

A catalogue record for this book is available from the National Library of New Zealand.

ISBN 978-0-14-377308-5

The assistance of Creative New Zealand towards the production of this book is gratefully acknowledged by the publisher.

creative nz
ARTS COUNCIL OF NEW ZEALAND TOI AOTEAROA

penguin.co.nz

FSC
MIX
Paper from responsible sources
www.fsc.org   FSC® C101537